It's Good to Have a GRANDMA

Maryann Macdonald

illustrated by
Priscilla Burris

Albert Whitman & Company
Chicago, Illinois

In loving memory of Mary B. Mooney
and Anna Vanderwerp—MM

For Blanche, Isabel, Judy, Rosario, Harriet, Lily,
and all you sweet grandmas I know and love—PB

Library of Congress Cataloging-in-Publication data is on file with the publisher.

Text copyright © 2019 Maryann Macdonald
Illustrations copyright © 2019 Priscilla Burris
First published in the United States of America in 2019 by Albert Whitman & Company
ISBN 978-0-8075-3676-6 (hardcover)
ISBN 978-0-8075-3672-8 (ebook)

Printed in China

10 9 8 7 6 5 4 3 2 1 WKT 24 23 22 21 20 19

Design by Aphee Messer

For more information about Albert Whitman & Company,
visit our website at www.albertwhitman.com

100 Years of Albert Whitman & Company
Celebrate with us in 2019!

It's good to have a grandma,
because grandmas aren't in a hurry.

They have time to catch lightning bugs
and to skip
and to blow bubbles.

"What's the rush?" my grandma always says.

Grandmas know things.

They remember the way the world was a long, long time ago, before you were born.

They can tell you what cars and telephones were like
way, way back when they were little.

Grandmas help,

because sometimes moms
are too busy to go sledding

or jump in the waves

or fly kites.

Grandmas let you help too.

They let you shine their glasses.

They let you feed the cat.

If you spill your milk by accident, grandmas say,
"Never mind. Everyone spills things sometimes."

If you make cookies, grandmas always eat at least one.

Here are some things grandmas like:
seashells,
flowers,
stars.

They know the names of some of them.

If you drop popcorn into the cracks in the couch, grandmas don't yell.

They never say, "You'll spoil your dinner," either.

If you want blue frosting on the cake, grandmas say, "Sounds good to me."

They never recycle your pictures,

even the splotchy ones.

Grandmas like to take you places,

like the beach, and berry picking,

and on the roller coaster too.

When they take you to work,
they make sure you meet all their friends.

Grandmas love shopping.

They can spend hours looking at goldfish
   and lightsabers
       and jewelry boxes with fairies inside.

They know choosing takes time.

I read to my grandma.

She reads to me too.

Sometimes we go swimming together.

Once she showed me how
to jump off the diving board
and touch the bottom of the pool
with my toes.

Grandmas don't mind waiting for the ice cream man.

"Yippee!"
they yell, when
they hear his bell.

My grandma likes to eat hot dogs on the street too.

She buys one for each of us.

We hate sharing.

One time my grandma helped me bury my parakeet.

We put Coco in a shoebox and dug a hole in the backyard.

Then we held hands and said all the nice things
we could remember about her.

We sang a song we made up.

Some names grandmas call you are:

Honeybear.

Sweet Potato.

Angel-pie.

Precioso.

Here are the things on my grandma's desk:

A magnifying glass with a silver handle.

A shiny paperweight.

Pictures of me, Mom, Grandpa, and Aunt Ali.

Here are the things in her handbag:

Keys on a sparkly chain.
A telephone you can play games on.
Lipstick and mints.

My bed at Grandma's house has twinkle lights.

It has a soft blanket too.

On rainy afternoons, Grandma and I make a tent under her table.

At night we play flashlight tag.

In the morning we make
cinnamon toast together.

We tell each other our dreams.

I don't remember when I didn't have a grandma.

I guess I always did.

We miss each other when we're apart.

When she calls I say, "I miss you, Grandma."

"I miss you more," she says.

Sometimes we send postcards.

My grandma has been to lots of places.

Paris is her favorite.

"Someday I'll take you there," she promises.

"What's the rush?" I say.

Grandma winks at me.

"Race you to the swings," she says.